NODDY
and the
RUNAWAY WHEEL

Illustrated by Wink

Purnell

Now one day when Noddy was coming back from Humming-Top Village, he heard a loud POP! His little car began to sway about, and Noddy stopped at once. What had happened?

"Oh dear—a puncture!" said Noddy, as he bent down to look at the wheel. "In my back wheel— what a nuisance. Thank goodness I've my spare wheel with me!"

Well, it wasn't long before Noddy took off the punctured wheel, to put his spare one in its place. He was so busy that he didn't see little Ben Bunny peeping at him . . .

He didn't see Ben standing the old wheel up,

and giving it a push. Oh dear — down the hill rolled the wheel, bumpity-bump! Now for a fine run!

Noddy finished putting on the spare wheel, and then looked round for the punctured one. It wasn't there!

"Where are you, wheel?" he said. "Where have you hidden yourself?"

Aha! Ben Bunny could tell you, Noddy.

The wheel is a long way away, with Ben running after it. It is bumping along at top speed, having a lovely time.

It met Big-Ears on his bicycle, and almost bumped into him, but Big-Ears JUST managed to ride into a ditch. He fell off, bump! How cross he was!

"That looks like one of Noddy's car-wheels!" he said, staring after it.

"Oh, my goodness, it's going to run into the milkman's cart. Stop, wheel!"

On went the runaway wheel, and BANG! It went straight into the milkman's cart. Bottles flew up in the air, and milk spouted all over the place.

The milkman was very angry. "Come back!" he

yelled to the wheel bumping happily off.

"Look out—the Skittle family are coming along. Look out, wheel!"

Down go the Skittles as the wheel runs right into them—bump and roll, bump and roll! Sally Skittle is most surprised.

It didn't stop. It ran straight at the poor Wobbly-Man and over he went—but he didn't fall down. No, he wobbled to and fro and then stood up straight.

"What hit me?" he said, in surprise. "I've got quite a dent in my middle!"

He stared after the wheel and gave a shout.

"Look out, Mr. Plod—hey, look out!"

Mr. Plod was standing in the street, directing

the traffic. The wheel came bounding towards
him, and bumped him right over. He was MOST
surprised.

There was soon quite a crowd round poor Mr.
Plod. Mrs. Tubby Bear helped him up.

"That's Noddy's car wheel," she said. "Little

rascal, letting it run away like this! I nearly got knocked over with it too! He must have sent it rolling down the hill."

"And he knocked me, and my milk-cart right over!" said the milkman, crossly.

"And us too!" said the Skittles.

"And that wheel tried to bump me over!" said the Wobbly-Man. "Look at the dent in my middle. Hark, what's that—parp-parp!"

It was Noddy coming along, hooting, looking for his runaway wheel. How surprised he was when Mr. Plod took hold of him and lifted him angrily from his car! "Noddy, how DARE you send one of your car wheels rolling down the hill?" said Mr. Plod, sternly. "It knocked heaps of people over, me as well. How DARE you do such a thing?"

"I didn't, didn't, didn't," said Noddy, in

surprise. "Oh, don't lock me up, Mr. Plod, please don't!"

But Mr. Plod marched him away, and the little car said "parp-parp" very sadly indeed.

Look at Noddy sitting all by himself in a tiny cell, feeling very sad. Outside he can hear his

little car hooting softly. It has run after him!

But who is this coming along through the village? It's Mrs. Bunny, with naughty little Ben Bunny!

"Please, where is Noddy?" she says. "Ben has done something very naughty!"

Mrs. Bunny saw Mr. Plod and went to him.

"Mr. Plod, my little Ben Bunny did a dreadful thing this morning—he rolled Noddy's car wheel down the hill! I hope it didn't knock anyone over, Mr. Plod."

The policeman frowned at Ben Bunny.

"So it wasn't Noddy!" he said. "It was you! And I've locked up poor little Noddy!"

Mr. Plod brought Noddy out, and pointed to Ben Bunny. "He rolled away your wheel!" he said. "Bend over, Ben Bunny. I'm going to give you a very good smacking!"

"No, no," said Noddy, "he's only a very little Bunny. Let him go!"

Mrs. Bunny was so glad. She took Noddy to the dairy and bought him an enormous ice-cream!